Gloom & Glow

by Tobias Reckermann

translated by Amy Hammack Turner

Gloom & Glow
by Tobias Reckermann
ISBN: 978-1-913766-42-9

Cover Art by David Rix

Publication Date: November 2025

Vision

Voice

Veracity

Contents

Nachtland

Marla wages a methodical war against dust. Today, it is more than that, it is a ritual. In her hands, the vacuum cleaner becomes a ceremonial staff as she clambers after the giant moth fluttering in the window. The dust spreading throughout the apartment seems to come from its wings. Marla is about to suck the creature up when she pauses and opens the window instead, waiting until the moth finds its way out into the light. She watches it go.

Marla's thoughts do not belong to this day. She thinks of the date she needs to cancel, of shopping, of a trip in the sunshine. Profane things, which she pushes aside. She closes the window and resumes the grim ritual, which must be built into humanity's genetic code.

Panzer has retreated into his room, shut the door and is listening to gloomy cello music. He feels it deeply and it vibrates on his frequency. The big guy has a tender heart.

Despite the vacuuming and the cello, the apartment is quiet, feeling empty and at the same time full again. Merlin sits in the living room, still and silent. After Marla has washed him, he wears the motorcycle jacket, jeans and sleeveless shirt that everyone knows him in. His long hair, his long hands. We thought about what he should take with him, and of course it's his drumsticks, now in his jacket pocket, and the snare drum. Panzer played with him so many times, guitar to Merlin's drums, though he is not a real musician like Merlin.

Merlin's band already knows. Hanna called them all this morning and will accompany them later.

We thought about who should take him and there is no family we know of. There are friends, the band, but we live with him, know him, love him too, and that's why we'll do it. Marla knew him first and lived with him for a while years ago when they were both new in town. They have always been friends. Panzer was there at his first concerts. For him, Merlin is a cornerstone of the world.

We need a car for the trip and Hanna borrows the band's ancient Granada. Merlin shall feel as if he were going on tour. We'll be in front, he in the back. But not until tomorrow.

Hanna cried, could never hold back tears. Why should she? In contrast to Marla's dryness and coolness, she is a hearthstone and overflowing water.

So we can use the station wagon for the next few days, the band drives it here. Guitarist and singer Marko and bassist Aristide get out in a cloud of cigarette smoke. Hanna turns off the sound system and the stoner rock falls silent. They come in and the two musicians cautiously go to Merlin in the living room and sit down with him. Hanna and Marla meet in the kitchen, hug, and then make coffee.

Panzer peeps out of his room and walks over to the band and Merlin. Everyone is quiet, restrained in their gestures. Two acquaintances of Merlin, who live down the street, come in. More friends will arrive in the next hour. Everyone visits Merlin, some stay with him, others stand around in the kitchen afterwards, drink coffee, water, beer and talk about the usual things. Marla is glad for the distraction, sits down briefly on a chair at the kitchen table and smokes while Hanna massages her shoulders. Panzer hardly says a word, at some point fetches his guitar and plays with Marko and Aristide, who have brought instruments. Kuf, who hasn't played for a while, drums on Merlin's djembe. The jam is in a minor key and becomes fast and loud in places, but soon lowers again. Marko starts to sing. Everyone listens for a few minutes before the conversation resumes.

The afternoon is grey and damp, but nobody turns on the lights until Hanna finally lights candles. Whoever looks at Merlin in their glow sees shadows emanating from him, stretching out and contracting against the wall behind his back, as if Merlin were dancing.

Others take over the instruments so that the music continues. More guests arrive, some leave. Many have brought something to eat and the kitchen fills with food. Hanna can't swallow anything, looks pale and thinks of the times she laughed with Merlin, sometimes argued with him, and remembers that when he was with Marla, he didn't know how to make jambalaya. She taught him.

Marla sits with him and holds his hands in hers. She thinks of many things, feels anger that she wants to push away but cannot. She thinks about tomorrow and the journey we're going to take.

As evening falls, many of the people leave. The band stays, the friends stay. Panzer is drunk and plays wrong notes. Marko takes the guitar from him, curses, and goes into the kitchen with Aristide to gain some distance. It goes on like that, everyone approaches, searches for space, stays close. Even those who leave stay in our thoughts.

The night is long for the few who remain. Stories about Merlin circulate, about gigs and women, collections of empty beer bottles that filled the Granada, arguments about where the scars on his neck come from. About him as a person, lover, enemy and above all as a musician.

A hangover dominates the morning until we get Merlin into the car and Marko and Aristide recede in the rearview mirror, tiny, out of sight. The world seems to know where we are going. The day is strangely quiet. You can tell that people who look in know or at least suspect. The city, the driveway, the country road, the soft rain, and grey sky that finally tears open and lets the sun through. We pass or drive through villages, listening to the band's last album. Merlin usually drove the Granada himself. Thousands of kilometres, to Greece, Italy, Spain, always to small performances in clubs, with just enough space for a three-person line-up, the drum set, without the toms, the small PA system, a couple of guitars, the bass, mics, cables—equipment that you can also use to play on the street.

There is room for three in the front. Panzer, who doesn't have a licence, sits in the passenger seat, cigarette lighter close at hand. Marla and Hanna take turns at the wheel.

Then the forest, the narrow road, two bridges over tiny rivers, no more people. We are there.

Nobody says a word for a while. We just listen. Watch. It is Nachtland, the night country, but hardly looks different. Trees, bushes, wild meadows, birds, just no people, no street signs. Asphalt so old that nature erupts through potholes. Side roads leading who knows where. Hanna drives slowly. "Do you know the wood engraving in which the old man carries his wife on a crate on his back?"

Panzer growls: "Yes." Marla: "Yes." We have the same thought, the same picture before our eyes. It dates from the thirteenth or fourteenth century. The old man walks with a stick, bent low. On his back is the frame in which he carried wood all his life, now holding his equally old wife, whose arms hang limply at her sides. Her head tilts to one side. Lines edging a darkness that spreads like shadows cast by the two people suggest a path taken through life, from here into the beyond.

We turn off the music, in order not to disturb anyone, or draw attention to ourselves, although the latter is, if not impossible, then unlikely.

We pass standing stones brooding in fields, a house with empty holes for windows. Others stopped here, did what they came to do, turned back without driving any further, without going deeper in. We continue on our way.

It is evening and red light spreads on the grass. Panzer calls, "Look!" and points to a ridge that rises to the left of the road. A figure sits on top. A person whose gaze crosses the street. Hanna, exhausted, stops at the edge and we look up at him. Motionless, he sits with his back straight and his head raised. We get out of the car.

There is no path up and we fight our way through tall grass. He is sitting on a chair. On closer inspection we notice the rope that ties him to the backrest, and as Panzer goes around him, he sees the rod sunk in the ground, the ribbon tied around the forehead and the rod so that the head doesn't droop. It's been here a long time, weathered, mummified. Insects, maggots, and birds have fed on him and created a morbid work of art. His bones stick out. From below, we saw an invitation, but now face an eyeless watchman. We can't leave Merlin with him. It's like the houses in Nachtland. They are not made for visitors, especially not for permanent guests. Where the dead have been put in graves, the earth is sealed, but so are the houses, like the lips of the dead themselves, like their eyes.

We become aware that we are under a spell that keeps the living silent. This makes Panzer restless and Marla nervous. Hanna, on the other hand, simply begins to cry and is the first to turn away from the sight, back to the road. She is sitting in the car when Panzer and Marla reach it, and starts it before they both get in. We had to come this far to understand. This is the land of night, the land of the dead, where the living are only shadows that fade with the brief light of day.

We must stay here overnight. In the moving car, we are not comfortable with the thought, especially since we want to go deeper.

"Where are we going?" asks Marla, as if there could be an answer to the question. None of us know our way. Panzer has already been here twice, but took different entrances, different roads. Hanna once came across the border in a boat when she was a child.

"I had a dream about a river," she says. "Maybe we will find it tomorrow."

Tomorrow. A night in this country. We stop when it gets dark but don't dare to get out. We feel watched, even more so because we know that there is nobody here that can watch us. Just the animals.

Life withdraws, turns off the lights in every room and leaves the body through the back door that it has always suspected, always searched for, and ultimately found. It is a quiet retreat, an eternal goodbye, the memory of a dream out of silence, of a place without space or movement. As envoys with our freight, we hear the silence, see the immobility. Both touch us. In this country, people have built houses and roads, created places, but always as hurried guests, prepared to turn around and flee, should the breath strike, grab them with clammy hands. You can feel it. We are all fascinated by it.

Sleep feels like forgetting. Since we're each only half asleep, we remember half of what we've seen. We expect a sudden movement in the back of the Granada, Merlin with drumsticks in his hands, beating out a marching song for his bones on the snare drum. The bones want to find their final place for themselves. Everyone can go home to one last place. A very last place.

The morning is as grey as the day before. Marla drives. The fuel gauge answers her question from yesterday. We can't go any further than our car brings us, with enough fuel to return.

Marla takes a side road, later a right turn instead of a left, following her instincts. The condition of the road, worse and worse with every kilometre, provides a second limitation. We can only go as far as Nachtland lets us. They say people walk through this country, perhaps even live in Nachtland. These people, if they exist, lean towards death. But we want to go home, although the temptation to stay increases with every kilometre inward.

Marla thinks of the years with Merlin, as a couple, then as friends, and all the events and opportunities that made up those years. At no other time would she have remembered so much. It is as if Nachtland has stored all these memories and distributes them like food to a starving person. Apart from the memories, Marla has nothing left. She looks at the road and sees completely different things. She brakes sharply, brings the car to a stop. "I'm not going any further."

Panzer turns his face to her questioningly, but there is no need to ask the question. Hanna points to a place to the right of the road where willows stand close together. "Maybe there."

We take Merlin out of the car. He seems very light now and Panzer picks him up like a child. Marla follows with the snare drum in her hands. Hanna comes last with the drumsticks, then pushes in front of the others and explores a depression that turns out to be a lea. You can hear water. Soft splashing. Only by following our ears do we come to a clear, narrow stream flowing through the grass near the willows. "That's it," says Hanna, "I saw him here."

Now we really say goodbye. In Hanna's dream, Merlin sat cross-legged with his back to her and a view of the water, holding the drumsticks in his hands and the drum on his lap. That's how we leave him behind. His torso leans over the drum.

When we are beyond the trees, we hear the rattle of the snare drum.

Marla wonders whether it could be the wind in the drum's wires. Panzer walks faster. Hanna laughs, nervous now, because there is no satisfactory explanation.

Marla stops for a moment, starts to turn around to look, but then gives in to the impulse to escape.

When we get to the road, we don't pause. We get into the car, Marla back in the driver's seat, and return home. As fast as the road allows. You must turn back before it's too late.

Further out in the country, there are supposed to be cities from very ancient times. Nobody goes that far anymore. Nobody believes the old legend of Rauhand, the king of Nachtland, and his riders. And yet, as we flee, we feel a pull from behind. Panzer looks back once and for a moment thinks he sees something moving at the vanishing point of the road.

He turns up the volume, and we drive to Merlin's music.

Machina Obscura

Blank woke up within the dream, wide awake in an instance, sensing someone with him in the room and paralysed with fear. He was sitting in an armchair with his back to whatever moved in the cold, night-dark, sprawling room. He saw the outlines of a window and door leading outside, too far away to be reached quickly. Faint looming faces with black eyes watched him from paintings on the walls. The air was still, like the bars of a cage. Blank hardly dared breathe, hearing the too-loud pounding of his own heart, feeling the frosty sweat on the nape of his neck, hard as iron, like a pole drilling into his skull. He feared that his arms, resting at his sides, might be visible to whatever was making the sound of tearing wood, but moving them would be even more dangerous. Tearing wood screeched, crackled, and crunched as if the house the room belonged was straining in its very core. With panic-wide eyes that couldn't find enough light and let in too much of the dark, and with ears painfully open, Blank measured the distance to the door and listened to advancing steps, a giant's steps clashing against the walls, listened to hate-filled breath sucked between the floorboards.

Passing time grew into a load on his exhausted body. With nothing moving in front of him and everything that happened behind his back—and what happened there!—carried forward into his rigid bones by the shaking floor, Blank sat until sleep overcame his terrified body.

When Blank arrived at work, his boss's first words were: "You have to see this, it's totally crazy!"

The two shared a strange affection for weird stuff from the Internet. So, with coffee in hand, but still in his jacket, Blank sat at the desk, on the office chair already warmed by his boss. He waved the screensaver away with the mouse and followed the eager instructions to click the inbox's first email. Looking over his shoulder, his boss chortled. "Better put down the coffee. Woah!"

It wasn't the usual spam—nothing to open, just a video that began to play on its own. Blank saw immediately what his boss meant. As the contents loaded, an image in colonial style emerged—dusty, age-spotted photography framed like an Old Master's oil painting, with Fraktur lettering on the edge. The camera zoomed in slowly from above, approaching the streets of a City After the

Rain, a ghost town that seemed to have grown from the weathered, furrowed earth. A figure came into view, growing larger, a person who at first had merged with the abraded buildings but now stood out clearly despite a coat the same mud-and-slate colour as the surroundings.

Now Blank noticed the sound, gradually swelling into a vibrating roar. Tension grew in his dream-fogged mind, tightening his cheeks. Abruptly, the figure filled the screen. Beneath the hood, Blank saw an angelic face, dazzling alabaster with spellbinding eyes. As they came nearer, the eyes burned with beauty. When the screen showed only the eyes, the pupils were revealed as empty but at the same time full, the deep black of oceanic trenches. The iris around each filled-in hole was not an iris. The eyes had been painted on white skin, around pupils like sphincters clenched into fists. The beauty shattered in a nauseating explosion, and the picture collapsed back into its frame and froze.

"Whoahh!" he cried out, spine shuddering, goose pimples prickling his skin. "Shiit!" As he turned, he saw his boss's gaping mouth transform into a triumphant grin. "Oh yeah! That'll go viral for sure."

Both tried to hide how deeply what they had seen unnerved them. They chatted about how the eyes and landscape must have been rendered and speculated about the design of the transition in the middle of the video clip. The style reminded them of this and that, the sound was like another video from some site or another. Both laughed a lot, though it didn't sound like laughter. Under any other circumstances, Blank would have replayed the video, but neither of them suggested that, though the boss had already seen it twice. Something spiny sat in their guts.

"Someone already called twice this morning, but hung up," the boss said. "Call them back, okay?"

"I will." Blank sipped his coffee, turning his mind to work. Taking off his jacket, he picked up the phone and redialled the number. A static hum followed the ringtone, then a sound he had never heard before, like a siren. After that, the call was dropped. Puzzled, Blank tried to call again. This time, he heard only the hum, no siren, then the lost connection. Supposing that the number was the problem, he looked it up on the Internet. He didn't recognise the area code, and the search engine didn't either. Then the phone rang again, and he took the call and heard a click as the caller hung up. It was the same number—some trouble with the device or the provider or whatever.

After the distraction, with the inbox still open, he felt a silent urge to look at the message and decided to wait for the caller to call again. Blank scanned the email: Machina Obscura, the headline in Fraktur, like an old book title. The background colour and texture reminded him of antique wallpaper. Under the frame of the video, he found contact data including a phone number, beginning with that same unfamiliar area code. On closer inspection, it was the same number that was on the office phone system.

"Fuck!" This was getting weird. Blank put the phone down on his desk, looked at it, looked at the email and then at the phone again.

"What's up?"

"They called?"

"Who called?" The boss came over.

Blank pointed at the screen. "Them!"

"It's witching hour." That was their code for 'hoax', for 'fake', but also for 'still, maybe not a fake'.

"Really," Blank said, "the number, here." He pointed at the phone's display, then at the number in the email.

"Come on. You dialled it."

"No, I didn't. See?" Blank showed him the number that had been recorded early in the morning, before he had arrived. They looked at each other, mouths agape. "Witching hour!"

Blank was distracted at work, always feeling those eyes drilling into him, or rather sucking him in. The siren had done the same thing, pulling at him like the zoom in the video. He used his break to research the site, not daring to simply click on the link in the email. He couldn't find it anywhere, even on social media, where you could usually find anything—bloody memes, horror clips, cheap decapitation gifs and chat about cadavers—the sort of thing he and his boss obsessed over, that was shared in a dozen groups and then shared again. Still more sites could be found on the dark web, some taking the whole thing very seriously, real horror sites with real corpses and—if you liked—real spectres and demons.

It didn't feel right to share the message. He sent it only to himself, posting just a screenshot to sites where someone might be able to identify its origin. Nobody knew anything and everybody said it was creepy. He spent hours after work searching for paths in uncharted territory that might lead to the obscure machine. This sort of activity pulled Blank away from the world, making it difficult to look into normal peoples' eyes. He feared they could see what he had seen, a reflection on his retina. Better to stay alone, associating only with those who shared his interests, his boss and a few others that they knew. They were, in a strange way, monsters—not because of anything they did, but because of what they watched. And this might be the biggest appeal.

If Blank had a girlfriend, life could get complicated. Some women saw beauty in this sort of thing, but most lost interest when it came to stuff like torture, unless they were already psycho. Snuff films, cannibals, dismemberment … he'd probably have to quit all that. Not that it would be a problem to give it up.

In comparison, the recent message was harmless, just tension and style, with no obviously shocking elements at first glance. The volume had not increased with the switch to full screen, and there were no surprises in the video after that. The connection with the phone call came in later. That left the overall style, which was what had appealed to Blank. Tripping on violence was methadone, like wilful intoxication with junk. Violence was just porn, a hardcore substitute for the real thing, the well-crafted subtle horror, which was rare or achieved with cinema-effects that were repeated too often.

The after-effects of too much exposure to his screen's blue light kept Blank half-awake and brooding for hours. When he finally fell asleep, it seemed that only seconds passed before he awoke in a cold, dark, dusty room with noise behind him. He sat in the armchair, which he recognised from another dream. In front of him, floating in the dark, eyes stared at him from the faces of the paintings. The door and window were once again just too far away for him to jump up and reach them. He was paralysed by fear and his heart hammered loudly, his breathing stalled and something scratched and screeched behind him.

The cracking steps moving toward him at last turned aside, and whatever made them pushed against the walls like an unseen giant imprisoned in a barn, breathing heavily. The fiend sucked air between the floorboards and through rifts in the wood, making Blank's hair stand up like ice-cold bristles at the nape of his neck and sending pain down to his last vertebra. His chest felt like an iron cage.

His eyes consumed darkness. The house vibrated with the blows. The steps moved away, but not far enough that Blank dared try anything. As time passed, Blank realised that he must be awake, not dreaming, but really sitting in this pit. That nearly stopped his breathing, but time went on in this continual state of shock, sapping his strength. Exhausted, he eventually fell asleep in the armchair.

In the morning, Blank's reflection in the mirror looked like a corpse. He had slept badly and woken up frequently, with a continual stream of pictures and thoughts.

It was a busy day at work, but he hardly woke up. During break, it hit him hard. In the dim afternoon light, with his collar up and the wind in his hair, Blank abruptly remembered last night's dream and his heartbeat jolted. And now he was wide awake, remembering the scene of that dream, dark shadows before his eyes, cold to his bones, hearing the clatter of the steps and ruckus raised by the thing in the house.

Blank swallowed. His pulse was too fast, his breathing too shallow, but it was day, and it was no dream that he was sitting in the wind nervously looking forward to meeting Kat for coffee after work. He had a date with a damned attractive woman who made him feel warm whenever he saw her. With some effort, he replaced the memory of the dream with eager anticipation of the date, then went back inside and managed to keep both in the background and to concentrate on his work.

After work, at the coffeehouse, Kat saw something in his eyes that he wanted to keep hidden out of shame. She was beautiful and her gaze made him feel that he was wearing the face of a monster. His side of the encounter was more than awkward. The whole time, Blank felt his skin folding into the wrong lines, unintended words coming out of his mouth, sitting like a stranger with this woman that he hoped to impress. They lost the thread of their conversation, or maybe there never was a thread, just loose ends leading nowhere. Though she was a few years younger, he felt like a clumsy teenager with a sophisticated woman. Because she didn't run away screaming, he stumbled through his lines until their brief parting hug and "see you soon."

Afterwards, he sat all evening, hollow and ashamed, not even looking at the Internet, only out the window into the dusk. Finally, overtired, Blank fell asleep on the couch.

He woke up in the cold dark room again and spent another horrible night there, though there was one change. The following morning, he remembered the dream, not only last night's, but also the previous ones, realising that he had dreamed the same dream over and over. He sighed into the mirror, took a hot shower, still feeling cold from the night, and asked himself what to do next.

He went to work, came home for the evening, and dreamed again. This time, Blank knew about the previous nights and was aware of being trapped. His body was rigid with fear. Nothing in the dream was different. Again, he heard the thing's steps and the noise, which he now believed could arise from an earthquake, shattering the house's foundation.

And in the morning, he knew with icy clarity that he had not been dreaming. The room was real, and so were the darkness, the paintings, the unreachable way out and, most important of all, the monster. Convinced without a doubt of an unexplained reality, Blank lived in the abyss of madness or beyond. His reality was worse than madness. He was sane, yet some process that he didn't understand abducted him into hell every night.

He could have talked to his boss, but that wouldn't have helped. He looked at Blank as he would have looked at a skull, with black rings around his eyes, and didn't say anything. If they hadn't had to serve customers, Blank might have said something, but they had too much to do for him to broach the subject of a couple of bad nights.

But a couple of nights became many.

After a week, Blank went to a doctor for a prescription for tranqs, because he was a wreck all day and didn't want to lose his job. He didn't look for a psychiatrist because he didn't consider himself mentally ill. He felt unsettled, shattered, exhausted, drained, stalked, tormented, terrified and yet not at all insane.

The tranqs helped him sleep. The nightmare—Blank didn't want to call it by any other name—still haunted him every night but with the help of the drug, he fell asleep in the armchair sooner. In the daytime, his life improved. He no longer looked like a corpse, though he still felt like one.

It was enough for him to function, nothing more. He gave up meeting friends, making conversation, having fun and feeling happy. He met Kat once, by chance, and they talked a little. He felt as if he was speaking from behind a curtain, as she drifted away from him on the other side. No "see you soon" this time.

One day, Blank stayed on the train, all the way to the end of the line, then back again to the other end, finally getting off at his stop the third time around. He went home in the dark, where only his computer's blue light illuminated the apartment. He felt cold, turned off, on hold. Real life happened late at night. With his own private horror, Blank no longer needed any from the Internet and felt no enthusiasm when his boss showed him some.

Instead, he began to fight back against the nightly terror. If he wanted to get out of that room, he had to overcome his body's paralysis. In a weird way, that had become even more difficult with time, because Blank felt more and more disconnected from his body, which didn't really do anything. His frozen limbs were not under his control. He felt trapped in an immobile space, his own body. But he had a comforting thought: if it meant him harm, the thing moving behind him had had enough opportunity to sense him, to find him. This knowledge slowed his heartbeat, lessened his panic a little. He could breathe more calmly now and plan how to escape. He just had to move his knees, lean forward, get to his feet and run, push open the door—if it was unlocked.

At work, Blank got an email with the subject line *Machina Obscura* from a guy he knew. He had hardly thought about that lately. The message was just a link to a website, the back door of an arms shop, numbers, symbols, dot-org, several frames on wallpaper, all in the initial email's style. He found nothing to open, but hovering over a particular spot, the mouse revealed the script: *Machina Obscura*. Blank tried clicking on it, left, right, left, and finally held the left button down while going over the spot as if highlighting. The script remained, and then letters changed. Two words became three: *haec exposito es*. The frame expanded and filled the screen. A dark room became visible, just barely, and in the centre, a box's polygonal silhouette, like a speaker box with a large bass skin, like an antique radio. Blank was spellbound, his eyes captivated, and he became aware of a glow in the centre of that woofer or whatever it was, some white electrical flickering. A machine, but obscure, its purpose and function unknown.

He tried in vain to go forward or backward from this page. The only choice was to stay there or to exit entirely. Blank shut down the browser and when he restarted it, he was glad it just showed the welcome page.

This time, he didn't even feel like showing the email to boss and instead tried to forget it. There was enough to do. Blank kept anything private out of his mind and the day ran its ordinary course until it was almost time to leave, when he checked the office email once again and found a message from *Machina Obscura*. His hand shook as he opened it and saw a letter formatted as if for print, complete with letterhead: *Dear customer, your order has been dispatched and is due for delivery on …*, the next day.

He let go of the mouse and sank back against his chair's backrest. Who had placed an order? Who wanted such a thing? Blank didn't believe his boss would have done it, at least not without telling him. No way had he ordered an obscure machine himself.

As if covering up his tracks, Blank marked the email *unread*, shut down the computer and left the office without saying much, cold dread in his spine. He drove home trying not to think and went to bed determined to escape the damned armchair and the frigid room.

Not yet asleep, something like lucidity came over him. Since the first dream and the strange message from *Machina Obscura,* Blank had lived in a different world. A reality of horror had taken complete possession of him, in his waking hours and in his sleep. His consciousness now perched on the rim of the normality that surrounded other people. Everybody, even the most confirmed sceptics, took it for granted. That included Kat, his friends, his colleagues, his boss, even himself before waking up in that cold room for the first time.

He feared there was no way back to that normality, ever. The next day the machine would be delivered, by whatever obscure means, on whoever's demand, most likely on nobody's demand, just arbitrarily. To what destination did he expect to escape, when he finally got out of the room?

Blank fell asleep with this unanswered question in his head and whatever waited for him before his closed eyes.

Of course, he arrived in the dark room, with its impression of indefinite age. His eyes must have adjusted to the lack of light, because the contours stood out more clearly, and the eyes from the paintings shone brighter. Blank felt the portraits' presence along with the something lurking behind him. Not only did the chair armrests feel cold, not only did his breath hang in the air, though his senses' petrification hardened everything.

Panic rushed back and quickened his heartbeat. Blank felt the violent cracking of floorboards in his bones.

If it was at all interested in him, it could have tracked him down long ago. It was probably completely indifferent to him.

That made the difference. Blank leaned forward, tensed his legs, pushed away from the armrests, brought his weight over his feet, stretched his knees. A sensation of burning excitement filled him, fear that didn't paralyse him but urged him forward with rapid strides toward the door, as the cracking became even louder behind him. The door wasn't locked, and he pushed it ajar, leaped through, found himself outside.

He couldn't help turning around, but the door slammed shut, snapping into its frame like fossilised wood as Blank stumbled backwards. The house flooded his field of vision, a looming structure of wood or corroded stone. He turned away and ran, hunted by his own heartbeat.

The air was so dry it made his lungs cramp, so he couldn't run far, only stumble through the City After the Rain. Buildings and streets grew like stalagmites out of the ground or survived endless erosion, sanded down from the whole, petrified wood the same colour as the sky, bathed in grey light. No doors or window frames filled the openings, which looked like skulls' eye-sockets. Of all the absences, that of human beings was the strongest. Blank instinctively expected to hear the flapping wings and hunting calls of pterodactyls. Cowering, he trudged further, realising that he'd fled not to safety but to a place worse than the cold dark room. Dust and ashes hung in the air over the urban desert and he moved onward, onward, over the craters and debris of a dead planet. Now, at last, he recognised the landscape of the video clip. In *Machina Obscura*'s world, he approached a figure that seemed to have grown out of this timestreams' discarnate bones.

The eyes' gaze was the only presence and he the sole being to gaze upon. He saw the white face ahead, the beautiful eyes painted over bottomless pits, and he fell unanchored into the deep.

When Blank woke up, his room was bathed in grey light. Raindrops beat against the windowpanes. He lay drenched with sweat in his rumpled bed. Every bone ached as he stood up. He looked out of the window, saw the city grey with rain under a sky of slate and thought of work. Today, *Machina Obscura* would arrive unwanted, his conception of its drive and function only a frightening shimmer.

Ironclad

Striding along the platform, Manuel Wied doesn't look at the sponsors waiting in proud anticipation; he only has eyes for his beloved machine. His gaze wanders from the smokebox door to the firebox over the blackened boiler cover. He climbs up the iron rungs into the engineer's seat, nods to his machinist, checks the steam pressure gauge—the boiler is already heated—and without further ado, pulls the lever that lets steam flow into the cylinders. A jolt travels from the pistons via the drive piston and coupling rods into the man-high wheels. Manuel pulls on the steam whistle as the Ironclad starts to move, freeing the people assembled on the platform from its spell. Cheers and the hissing of the smoking monster's chimney fill the train shed. Manuel smiles as he feels the power of five hundred tons of awakened steel in his bones and muscles. The machinist, now just a boilerman ceding the place of honour to the chief engineer, takes charge of the tender and the firehatch.

In the firebox, hell's little vestibule, prehistoric fuel from primeval forests goes up in searing flames, becoming a hot gas that rushes through the pipes to exchange heat with the water in the boiler. Five hundred tons of heavy cast steel chugs over the rails, heading out of the station in a southerly direction, pulling no cars. Only the machine. The heart of fire beats. The chimney spews. Pressure builds up, pushes against the bolts and the joints. Stroke by stroke, the locomotive picks up speed.

"Manuel Wied promised great things—two hundred kilometres an hour, without cargo and on straight, level tracks. Two hundred! For a machine weighing five hundred tons, that was pure madness. Of course Wied and the machinist knew that the Ironclad could do much more."

"So was the maiden voyage just a show?"

"Partly, but it was really a test of steam distribution in the boiler, the reinforcement of the exterior, the couplings, the bolts and the joints, anything that can fatigue at high loads."

"But the sponsors knew nothing of the special alloys?"

"No, that was all kept under cover. The sponsors wanted a war locomotive, a battering ram as they called it. They simply meant a really fast, heavily armoured locomotive that could pull a full load and would be easy to maintain. With the Ironclad, cities could be levelled. But the name and all that was only politics. On the other hand, the alloys had military significance. They were developed under the code name *Algol*. The iron casters in Gotheim laughed at the outrageous cost, saying they might as well have built the Ironclad out of gold, but it was only a damned big heavy war machine. They laughed, but if you knew these men, you could tell that they were impressed."

"It must have seemed way too expensive to the sponsors too."

"It would have been, if the lion's share hadn't come from the military, secretly, from some imperial secret account. Basically, the point of asking for bids was just to be able to give the monster a long test run. They could have never gotten it from Gotheim to Cologne without attracting attention. But the launch took place behind closed doors. Only the partners knew what would leave the Gotheim station. They silenced the press with bribes and threats from the secret police. Later, there were rumours, because the Ironclad couldn't pass unseen through the city, but rumours could be handled."

"And military research enjoyed full public support then."

"Definitely!"

"It is still surprising that nothing leaked out from the iron casters."

"There were lots of secret projects in the steel industry, in the entire defence industry. Yellow

Cross and other chemical weapons were developed secretly. The factories kept a close eye on their workers, and knew who not to trust in delicate situations. They knew all the communists, the trade unionists, the pacifists. A careful division of labour took care of some problems, and unaligned foreign powers, for example Romanians, took care of others. It wasn't very hard."

"And you also implied that only Wied knew the function of certain details in the blueprints."

"He and his machinist knew. The improvements to the engine and the blastpipe that Wied developed were revealed later. And then there was the *Vril*. You see, the Ironclad was powered by steam, superficially. Right out of the manual-boiler, firebox, smokebox, cylinder, but Wied and the machinist planned something completely different."

"Vril, you say? Like what the Nazi's supposedly …"

"Used for their flying saucers, yes, but I don't know anything about that."

"Really? That surprises me. Weren't you later …?"

"I know nothing. Must I remind you of our agreement? We can't discuss that."

"Yes, but Vril? The Vril Society?"

"You know about it, do you? No you don't. You've heard about it and maybe made some clever guesses, but I'm telling you that is all in your imagination. The thing you're thinking of never existed. Vril is the name that Wied and the machinist used, because it fit."

"Excuse me, but I have to ask: You often speak of the machinist, but who was he?"

"Well, half of the puzzle's solution, that much is clear."

"But …"

"I don't know who the machinist was or even his name."

"Then …"

"I'll talk about the machine, if that's what you want. What I know, how I know it, and whether I really know anything is up to you to figure out, isn't it? If not, we can't go any further."

"Hmm, then what should I … OK, go on."

"The Ironclad went over two hundred kilometres an hour, even without the Vril. The speed was never officially recorded, but it was a little faster than the 002 and the Mallard. The fastest locomotive in the world, and five times the usual weight!"

"Unbelievable!"

"Certainly. But it was all kept secret. A few years earlier or in the twenties, it would have revolutionised everything. I mean *everything*."

"And the Vril?"

"The Vril. For Wied, that was the only reason to develop the Ironclad. It wasn't about breaking records or winning the war. He wasn't that sort of man. Manual Wied was a … visionary says too little. He was insane in the best sense of the word. He came from Schleswig, and it would have been easier for him to work on chemical weapons in the Kiel shipyard. But he went to Gotheim to build locomotives for Alen AG.

"The machinist must have showed up soon after, and the two men were always seen together. Wied, the slim young guy with striking grey eyes, who was only interested in blueprints, and the machinist, surely twenty years older, grey at the temples, with the aura of a man who had probably served overseas. At any rate, he was worldlier than Wied, though nobody in high society would have noticed him, more the sort of man who associated with iron casters and coal miners. Manuel Wied was well educated and was raised to be comfortable in ballrooms and at conferences."

"Somebody who could talk to financiers, I assume."

"Yes, that's right. If somebody was there who could translate his ideas, his enthusiasm shone through. Wied and the machinist worked together almost as if they were one person. Which is not to say that the machinist didn't have his own mind. You could see ideas behind his eyes, and mystery. The Vril is mystical, just as Bulwer-Lytton describes it in his book."

"By mystical, you mean occult."

"Only in the sense that it didn't reveal all of itself. The machinist had it under control, and Wied too, through him, but I don't think they really understood it. Because it's more than the science of the time, or even of today, could explain."

"Where did they get the Vril? Where did it come from?"

"Only the machinist knew. Wied had ideas about how it could be used, and how to accomplish that with engineering technology, but apparently he never asked where it came from. He understood the power that came from the Vril, and that was enough for him. He was not a natural scientist or a physicist."

"No Oppenheimer then?"

"No, more like Von Braun."

"Then was the machinist something like his Warsitz?

"Or the Mephistopheles to his Faust. Probably both, I think."

"That would make the Vril hellfire."

"Ha! Well, we can only speculate about that. In the novel *The Coming Race*, Vril is a force that is in everything or flows through everything, a primal or vital force, and these people, the Vril-ya, mastered it with their minds, telekinesis, telepathy, something like that. It could be used to heal or destroy, or awaken inanimate matter to life. Like I said, it's not the same thing, but to animate matter, that's exactly what Wied wanted to do."

"With the Ironclad?"

"The Ironclad itself."

"How ...?"

"The Ironclad was powered by coal and steam. There were some technological improvements, but it was basically like any other steam engine, locomotive, paddle steamer, steam roller, and so on. Hundred-year-old technology. But when the temperature in the firebox reached about thirteen hundred degrees Celsius and the Ironclad accelerated to more than two hundred kilometres an hour, the machinist added the Vril. Like an injection of nitrous oxide in an internal combustion engine. Or the Vril could have been there all along. The two people who knew never told. The acceleration to two hundred served as a test of the materials and construction under natural but extreme conditions. The rails were as much of an issue as the boiler. Everything, including wheels, axles and valves, were subjected to a really extreme force. Rails buckled as a result of the record-breaking trip. But the Ironclad held up.

"The true test came later in the war, on a route without civilian traffic, behind the western front. A mass of five hundred tons moving two hundred kilometres an hour means a tremendous amount of kinetic energy, and then the Vril was set free at thirteen hundred degrees Celsius. Suddenly there was additional thrust, as if the locomotive had been standing still and accelerated from zero to a hundred. The tachometer scale was useless. More than twelve hundred kilometres an hour. There was a bang as loud as Big Bertha firing right next to your ear. The Ironclad had broken the sound barrier. This time, the rails behind her looked as if Heimdall himself had battered them with his hammer. Bent and twisted like a spring behind the locomotive as it sped on, unbelievably unharmed. But Wied and the machinist had done the calculations and knew that the Ironclad wouldn't explode."

"That is ..."

"Fantastic. And true. All the exhaust blew out in one puff. There was not a drop of water left in the boiler and the coal had all been burnt. But the Ironclad kept going. She was slower, and one could believe she was only coasting, but she maintained a constant speed of one hundred and fifty, without a mote of coal dust or a drop of water. That was the Vril."

"..."

"You can't conceive of this, huh? So, earlier, the machinist might have locked the Vril in the firebox and fed it coal, and when it got hot as hell, the Vril flowed into the machine, the Ironclad, animated matter, living steel. And she is still alive."

"And now ...?"

"She is still alive. But she was not built for rails. The boiler did more than withstand the thrust ..."

"Where is she now? All this secrecy, the war, but she must still be somewhere, in your story."

"Not on Earth! The Ironclad was no longer a locomotive, after they took off her wheels and all. Wied and his machinist transformed the boiler into the central part of a ship. After the war. In the twenties. The alloys strengthened the hull sufficiently for her to operate in outer space. A living ship, which after an initial push to achieve escape velocity from Earth, could accelerate more under its own power and leap out of the solar system, far beyond Neptune at a speed of 670.3 kilometres per second, to fly to Perseus. With a constant acceleration of 1g, the mere 28 parsecs to Beta Persei is not far."

"Yes! Just a hop, skip and a leap away, when you think about it, but you know, I can't … with the best of intentions, I can't write anything about this. I know we made a deal, but wouldn't you rather tell me about your expedition to Tibet?"

The True Face

0

An entire wall of the room opens, not just a door or window. As always, a hundred rude faces peer in. Today they are quiet, waiting, for once not loud, just malicious, always malicious. But they can't do anything to me, they play no role; only their evil can cross the threshold, poisoning the room.

The story begins, always following the same course. They start to laugh at my fate, the tragedy, the inevitability of my failure. Always the same, always ending badly.

Characters appear. My mother, who seemed to have never noticed me among all her clients and her work as a realtor. Her face emerges from darkness, she speaks then fades again into darkness, vanishes. My father, the clown, always making dumb jokes without really saying anything. My ex-husband, who will never vanish from my life, although he was the one who destroyed our marriage. My supervisor, who treats me like an idiot. The pig with horns like bayonets and the tongue of fire. Other things, faces, streets, houses spin like the barrel of a revolver, discharge their powder, their lead.

I react, try to play my role correctly and give everyone what he, she or it needs to make sense of the whole. I hurry from encounter to encounter, always the focus of a hundred faces, the centre of their attention, the target of their mockery, their complaints, their ill will. I die, more than once, and stand up again. There is no other existence for me.

And the wall closes. Again it becomes dark and quiet and my breath stops.

1

I first saw my true face late in life, in my thirties. Until then, my whole existence was a lie. It makes me laugh that it all began in a self-discovery workshop, where nobody would expect such a transformation. I stepped into a magical moment of clarity, which has expanded continually since then.

I remember neither the tools or the materials, but they couldn't have been anything more remarkable than plaster of Paris and paste and paint. What happened in my hands is more important. My fingertips vibrated as I worked, as if resonating with my inner frequency and recording oscillations like seismographs, bypassing thoughts and intentions as they wielded spatula and knife and paintbrush. From the imprint of my false face, the real one arose. Eyes set far apart, just small round openings, brows like the outspread wings of a crow, the nose a sharp hatchet, almost a beak, cheekbones like a black helmet's red faceguard, with a black star in place of a third eye, the mouth vertical, like a toothy gate leading downward.

I don't believe in witchcraft but I was sure that this was a magical event, that I had stumbled unawares into what was more truly myself than I was. I seized this piece of reality and left the workshop without a word, the mask like a newborn child in my arms, unaware of my route until I found myself sitting on a park bench, from which my expanding gaze surrendered to the wholeness of the day. Everything had reversed itself. In my hands, the lies had become the mask, the mask the truth.

2

I had reason to smile because so much that had made my past life unbearable fell from me like flakes of burned paper and floated away. I didn't need to look at the mask to recall its features. It was mine, and as familiar as if I had seen it in the mirror every day of my life. What stopped me from smiling was that now I had shed my own lies, the much bigger lies of the world faced me.

I can't know if what I recognised had been apparent before, or had become visible through a new experience, perhaps my inner experience. It was a hot day and the sun stood in the sky, unhidden by clouds or haze. Its brightness burned over me, making all surfaces unbearably sharp.

There was something powerful about the glare, as if an eye had opened, under the sun, the eye of a sleeping spirit. The mighty blue of the sky, usually so impenetrable, was now threadbare, like a worn-out cloth. Shadow seeped through, flowing from the black eye. Above me, a darkness burst through the seams of the bright day, as though she was too big for her gown.

I still lacked a deeper understanding, so I sat rigid with fear and kept my eyes lowered, as though before a mighty ruler. I felt a sense of profound menace, and I cannot say anything but that knowledge crept up on me, that it seeped into me like water running uphill, until it reached the domain of my consciousness and took possession of it completely. An hour earlier I would have had to burn up in madness, but now I stood firm. I realised that even the cosmic night wears a mask—which we call the day!—hiding what lurks behind all things. Although I should finally have felt strong with my true face, I became infinitely small under that shadow.

3

I fled from the park and boarded a nearby train. As soon as I took a seat, I knew it was that white train that I dreamed about only in my wildest dreams, now completely real. The compartment was almost empty, holding just one or two other passengers, fewer passengers than the train in my dreams. It had to be on the track that lead into the darkness.

Who wants to visit a place that is not really a place? Looking at my reflection in the window, I wondered if anything at all existed beyond it.

My face taut, my gaze glided away, brushing the pale gentleman two rows ahead of me, who sat upright in a black suit, wedged in a collar and tie, and never turning his head. Only a slight vibration showed that the train was moving, no engine noise, no passing landscape, nothing. Other wagons in front and behind remained invisible, nobody coming in or out through the doors.

In this moment, I felt that a place where one stayed a long time could distance itself more and more from everything else, until one could no longer leave it. A place of its own, a domain of a consciousness, closed, hermetically sealed. The compartment could become a cosmos without connection, without exit, without vanishing point, existing only in itself.

Like the guardian of a secret treasure, I hid the mask under my jacket, boundlessly happy that I had not revealed it to the darkness of the sky. Seeing my true face would have given it power over me, but this way I was protected, as if by an assumed name or fake identity. I would be able to discover for myself the strength in my true form before I divulged it to anyone else.

I thought of the lying spirits of my mother, my father, my ex-husband, my supervisor, for the first time in my life happy that they protected me, giving credibility to my legend, standing like a maze in the way of the threat surrounding me.

4

The second face, which I wore in the compartment, found no trace of that third passenger whose presence I felt vaguely. Looking around me, I could only see the gentleman in the suit.

The train did not stop in a foreign country, or in a better place, it left me right outside my house. Its white steel illuminated the night like a lantern—was it night, or had the day just become invisible to me? A shadow lay on the dam and I saw the pale gentleman get out behind me. His gaze touched me, then he turned and walked away, his shadow with him. It was not the one I sensed, the third one who was like my own shadow.

The train departed into the darkness. I stood alone in front of the house where my ex-husband had lived with me, which was too big for me now that I was alone. The feeling of being accompanied slipped through the door with me. I took off my jacket that hid the mask, still with the uncomfortable sensation of being watched. A self-discovery workshop had brought me back to the place that was the haven of my self-doubt. The train had not carried me away but brought me back, proving that there was no way for me to escape. So I had no choice but to face the danger, however little I understood it, however much I was afraid, however much I doubted myself.

Though I believed I was not alone, the only thing I could do was to wipe away the lie and put on the mask, to claim my true face. Instead of turning on the light, I lit candles and bent over the jacket in their glow, opening it like the pages of a forbidden book. I took the mask in both hands, first holding it in front of me like a mirror, then turning it over to put myself behind that mirror.

5

The house, as I said, had belonged to my husband and me, had been our home. We spent happy days there, and later less happy, ordinary and increasingly tense days. Finally, our relationship fell apart and we filled the house with demonic energy. When I returned home from work in the evenings, it was as if I entered a mansion haunted by evil spirits, but the spirits were just the two of us. That changed after his departure.

There's a back door that leads into the garden. The first night after my husband left, something hit hard against the door from outside. It was not a knock, but a brutal thud that startled me out of my chair and out of my deep thoughts. Alone, I already felt vulnerable, and yet I assumed that it was something like a bird lost in the night.

I ran to look and when I opened the door, the threshold was empty, and the outside of the door was unharmed. Whatever had made the noise must have left on its own.

This was the beginning of a long series of bad nights. Every time I was ready to sleep long after nightfall, or long since asleep, the rumble and thunder repeated at the door. It was rarely over with a single strike like that first night. Usually, the hammering repeated dozens of times and I spent hours in fear. A supernatural fear, for neither the windows at the back of the house nor the open door itself had ever revealed anything that could explain this noise. My sleep became paper thin and soon I sickened physically. Grief and anger at my separation mingled with growing fear, and with the anger I increasingly felt at work, with the sense of insignificance in the sharp light of my parents' inattention, the swelling panic that finally arose from the impossibility of sharing my experience.

I did not have friends. As it turned out, all our friends took my husband's side, not mine. All this gradually took over the whole structure of my being, until one night something happened that brought it to the point of collapse.

<h1 style="text-align:center">6</h1>

The hammering began soon after ten o'clock. I had started drinking right after my arrival home. My head already felt like an eggshell from which a dreadful bird was starting to hatch.

The alcohol brought me across the threshold of fear, and I ran angrily to the back door, ripped it open after a wild blow, stepped out and yelled at the night to finally end this grotesque game. Because there was nothing there, I slammed the door and began to cry, howling, tearing at my hair, biting my fists, kicking at the door to drown out the thunder, cursing myself for my existence, my weakness, my pitiful soul.

I cowered against the wall beside the door, then dragged myself upstairs and into my bed and probably slept, or lost consciousness, until the door of the bedroom, which I had left open, slammed shut.

I awoke and sat upright in the dark. There was something near me that approached with bony throbbing on the floorboards. Out of complete darkness, a face thrust itself before my eyes. It was the head of a black pig, human-like and horrible, with steel bayonets for horns, and such small, black eyes. The upper part of the face seemed completely empty of emotion, though the eyes radiated intelligence. However, the lower part, the awful mouth, grinned at me and opened to unroll a tongue of flame. I do not know if I screamed, but the tongue stabbed into my mouth and I felt it enter my head, my brain, a rape of the cruellest kind. My ego, my mind, my soul itself was violently penetrated and all my will extinguished, the little black eyes looking coldly into mine.

I know that it stopped, that the being withdrew, leaving me burned and dying inside. For a long time, no thought could connect to this experience. I just lay there, like the ashes and debris of a looted and destroyed city, until finally morning came.

7

I locked myself up for six weeks in a psychiatric hospital and let myself be convinced that all this was an outgrowth of my inner condition, that my soul punished itself by fabricating demons.

In the months that followed, out of necessity, I resumed my job and reached out to my parents and even my ex-husband, who supported me generously when I felt so bad. Medications helped me endure my suffering, but I especially depended on not being completely alone. Spending only the lonely nights in the house, dazed by drugs, I heard no thundering at the back door, although I often dreamed of it. I had to return to my old life, because there was nothing else for me. I couldn't stay where I was. I mustered all the strength I could find for this experiment.

The workshop was the most recent attempt to build something out of the fragments of myself. I could not believe that I would be capable of another relationship, so I had to accept the fatal consequence of remaining childless. I lacked the courage to train for a new career. Selling the house and going away would require strength that I could not find in my inky soul. To move away from anyone who at least knew me would cut the last thread of my life.

These workshops, as well as all the counsellors that I clung to during this time, could only serve as a distraction. For a brief time, I tried to believe them, to believe everything would improve over time, I would find inner strength, my mind would clear up, new possibilities would open up, unexpected events would enable me to be a different person, feel joy, even love, and become whomever I wanted. However, the moment these crutches were set aside, my confidence crumbled. All promises faded to views from the soot-blackened windows of my inner house. Outside, children could play, and the sun could shine, but I could not leave that house.

I cannot say how I finally entered the magical moment in which everything seemed to change, in which I found my true face and the courage to put it on.

8

I look through these eyes for the first time and everything changes its shape. First my body mutates into a monster. I no longer wear the defenceless flesh of a woman, but the powerful limbs and features of a beast. Since my eyes are set on the side of my head, my field of vision is wide, but strangely divided into two. My hands form sharp claws and I feel black and red plumage wrap around me. The armour of a storm crow. The attitude of a warrior. The courage of a stronger self.

The house around me also assumes a different nature. All surfaces are now like the black skin of a gorilla. Under this skin, I hear and feel the pulsating current of dark blood.

In my worst dreams, I have seen the house, not as my abode, but as a gateway to hell. Hence the terrible hammering at the back door, the narrow path through the garden becoming the path the horde takes when it tries to enter the human world. Now I recognise the truth of my dreams. The house is both a sally port and a last obstacle. It holds the demons back, a castle against the onslaught of the horde, perhaps built by primeval guardians. It has either changed its shape with time or presents its own mask to people. I realise that we living people are rebels against the cosmic power of entropy. We challenge chaos, striving to annihilate the cold of the universe, grotesque in the eye of this primal power.

Instantly, the hammering at the gate is overpowering. No mere fists, but battering rams, smash against the door. The whole house roars and shakes; the walls tremble. And something else is there. My newly heightened sense of smell tells me someone is here in the house with me. It must be the one I brought in, invisible by my side. I smell fear, but also hate, something that may have come from powerlessness. Quick steps hurry down the hall behind the wall to my right and I jump out behind them.

9

In this naked reality, the house has new rooms, chambers like dark shells strung together in a chain. The long hall flows like a bloodstream, branching like the roots of an evil plant.

Listening, because my goal is already out of sight, I hurry on, losing track of what floor I'm on in the ascent and descent of many levels that flicker with each step forward, as if the cells of obscure organs pulse forward, then sink behind others into the occult. Stairs are shafts, windows are shields, doors are eyelids, muscles that close convulsively and open abruptly. Behind all this, something sucks with cold or hot hunger, implying depths that can lead to the hereafter, to other worlds.

If I were my false self, I would die of fear, but I am the hunter in this dungeon, I am the Minotaur in the labyrinth, I am the eagle in the air. I smell, I follow. I sharpen my claws on the leather of the walls. Whomever I follow cannot feel more at home here than I do. The dark star on my forehead ignites the fire of an additional sense that lets me know where in the house I am, in which direction I am going.

The one fleeing from me is on the way to the back door. Faster, I must move faster to prevent something irreversible. Shadows flee before me into the darkness of the chambers, behind doors that close themselves. Eyes that I think I recognise turn away and I hear little wooden feet tapping. Then a foul tooth breaks out of the black skin in front of me. I realise too late that it is part of a mouth that closes in front of me like an iron portcullis.

A scream breaks out of me, the screeching of a wild crow, and I spread out jaws and wings, slamming them against the teeth of the maw and smashing them, plunging through the mouth and falling behind the teeth into the larynx-like passageway. I roll over and jump up to confront what waits at the end.

10

The white figure of a woman stands in front of the door leading into the garden. That's me, trying to open the door to hell. My false self. Her shape is tattered, as if eaten away by moths, a shroud with my old face. I am still the hunter, but I realise with a start that it is she who accompanied me, who entered the house by my side. The lie is not broken but rather has its own life that does not need me.

One more profound truth hits me like a blow. My horrible journey started before I succumbed to the black pig, before the hammering on the back door came into my life, before I was left alone in this house, before I quarrelled with my husband, before I even knew him. Before all that was my youth, before my childhood, which from the beginning was a place of hell in which I, the false one, was forged. An ice-cold key, created solely for the purpose of opening the door to hell. This house is a body, yes, it is my body, and under the heart is a secret door that you cannot see in the light of the day, which would be best left closed forever, for chaos waits behind it. The killer pit. The darkest place from which all evil springs.

So my thoughts run through the hourglass of my remaining time. My false self unlocks the lock and lays her hand on the latch. I hear the howling behind her, the baying of the deep, the oozing desire for murder. One last leap carries me over the final part of the hallway and as the door is already open a crack, I crash against it with all my strength. The door slams closed and its frame trembles. All the beasts of hell scream furiously behind it as I collapse onto my shroud, which arches up under me like an inchworm.

10,000

I inhabit this house now, a beast at the threshold, a Cerberus at the gate to Hades, the silent guardian of hell. The house is my flesh. Its windows are both eyes and shields. I know what brews beneath me, where the door under my heart resists every night's onslaught.

Outside, day after day passes. I know the days are just the mask of the eternal night. I do not answer knocks on my door, the front door that opens onto the street. I do not let my parents or my ex-husband in. Instead, I moan loudly and hit the walls, which writhe in pain.

Nobody comes in here, through either door. Nobody! The old dreams do not return, neither the good nor the bad. I do not need them anymore. From time to time, a white train stops on the opposite side of the road, releasing passengers who disappear into the dark, picking up others and, I hope, taking them to a better place.

It's fine the way it is now. I think, soon my house will be abandoned and hardly recognisable. Maybe an inconspicuous ruin, maybe just a hill or tangled vegetation. Everyone must forget me and forget the house, but above all nobody must open the back door, through which the horror I saw in the sky tried to come into my world. So long as I am here and guard the path, nobody will do that.

I now think that what I have experienced has no beginning, or started outside of my time and experience. It is a play restaged over and over. So maybe the mask is not only mine, but part of a costume that must be worn by someone like me forever. It is not a tragedy that my own time forgets me here, but much more what you call a happy ending.

www.ingramcontent.com/pod-product-compliance
Lightning Source LLC
Chambersburg PA
CBHW051714180726
48283CB00004B/1338